Car Stars
PORSCHE
911

ROCHESTER PRIMARY SCHOOL
7440 JAMES ROAD SW
ROCHESTER, WA 98579

911 Carrera

Dash!
LEVELED READERS

Dash!
LEVELED READERS

Level 1 – Beginning
Short and simple sentences with familiar words or patterns for children who are beginning to understand how letters and sounds go together.

Level 2 – Emerging
Longer words and sentences with more complex language patterns for readers who are practicing common words and letter sounds.

Level 3 – Transitional
More developed language and vocabulary for readers who are becoming more independent.

abdopublishing.com

Published by Abdo Zoom, a division of ABDO, PO Box 398166, Minneapolis, Minnesota 55439.
Copyright © 2018 by Abdo Consulting Group, Inc. International copyrights reserved in all countries.
No part of this book may be reproduced in any form without written permission from the publisher.
Dash!™ is a trademark and logo of Abdo Zoom.

Printed in the United States of America, North Mankato, Minnesota.
092017
012018

Photo Credits: Alamy, iStock, Shutterstock
Production Contributors: Kenny Abdo, Jennie Forsberg, Grace Hansen, John Hansen
Design Contributors: Dorothy Toth, Neil Klinepier

Publisher's Cataloging in Publication Data
Names: Murray, Julie, author.
Title: Porsche 911 / by Julie Murray.
Description: Minneapolis, Minnesota: Abdo Zoom, 2018. | Series: Car stars |
    Includes online resource and index.
Identifiers: LCCN 2017939247 | ISBN 9781532120824 (lib.bdg.) | ISBN 9781532121944 (ebook) |
    ISBN 9781532122507 (Read-to-Me ebook)
Subjects: LCSH: Porsche 911--Juvenile literature. | Vehicles--Juvenile literature. | Cars--Juvenile
    literature.
Classification: DDC 629.2222--dc23
LC record available at https://lccn.loc.gov/2017939247

Table of Contents

Porsche 911

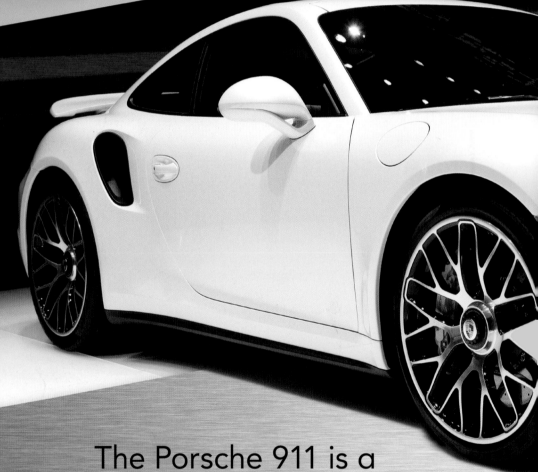

The Porsche 911 is a German **sports car**. It is very popular!

The first 911 came out in 1963.

Many 911 **models** have been made over the years. The 1989 Speedster was a convertible.

The 2017 911 Turbo S can go from 0-60 mph (0-97 kph) in 2.6 seconds. Its top speed is 205 mph (330 kph).

The 2016 911 Carrera S
Cabriolet is a convertible.
It sells for around $100,000.

The Look

The Porsche 911 has two doors. It has four seats.

It has a **sleek** body.
The corners are rounded.

A **spoiler** is on the back
of the 911 Carrera RS. It
helps the car stay on the
ground at high speeds.

All 911s have the engine in the back. This allows for quick starts and stops.

More Facts

- The 911s are Porsche's best-selling car.

- The 2018 GT2 RS is the fastest 911. It can go from 0-60 mph (0-97 kph) in 2.7 seconds!

- Porsche racing cars have won more than 24,000 races.

Glossary

model – a particular type or style of product.

sleek – smooth.

spoiler – a long, narrow, hinged or fixed plate that modifies airflow and thus improves the performance of a vehicle.

sports car – a low-built car designed for performance at high speeds.

Index

Online Resources

Booklinks
NONFICTION NETWORK
FREE! ONLINE NONFICTION RESOURCES

To learn more about Porsche 911, please visit **abdobooklinks.com**. These links are routinely monitored and updated to provide the most current information available.